O. Henry

Perfect

Three short plays adapted from
the works of O. Henry

by

DAVID J. MAURIELLO

ISBN: 978-0-9716853-1-4

Library of Congress Control Number: 2013920814

book production by
Great Life Press
www.greatlifepress.com

David J. Mauriello
12 Winship Drive
Wakefield, MA 01880

email: Djmrllo@aol.com
www.davidjmauriello.com

CONTENTS

About the Author.   v

Why "Perfect"?.   vii

The Perfect Fool.   1

The Perfect Stranger.   17

The Perfect Archer   29

Notes   53

ABOUT THE AUTHOR

David J. Mauriello is an award-winning playwright, author of the book *REMINDERS OF HOME, How To Remember Who You Really Are,* and is the Executive Producer of the movie JUST SAY LOVE.

> JUST SAY LOVE —"A strikingly elegant, moving and satisfying film. Truly a wonderful cinematic creation."
> —*TLA Video*

> SPIRITS WILLING — "sparkles, Mauriello proves a resourceful craftsman." —*The Boston Phoenix*

> BODY — "phenomenally well crafted script"
> —*Rockingham County News*

Much gratitude to the Players' Ring of Portsmouth, New Hampshire, for their unfailing dedication to promote original plays.

WHY "PERFECT"?

O. Henry (William Sydney Porter (1862-1910) wrote hundreds of entertaining tales. His perfection of the "twist-to-the-plot ending" and unique style make him a true American original.

His Christmas classic THE GIFT OF THE MAGI illustrates another reason for O. Henry's popularity; his representation of the common man and woman.

While adapting THE GIFT OF THE MAGI I more fully realized that O. Henry's dialogue with its delightful combinations of superlatives and malapropisms would be "perfect" when spoken for theater audiences.

Here is a sample of what some have labeled "ohenryisms."

On trying to understand women:

> "I tell you Andy, I never had the least amount of
> intersection with their predispositions. Maybe I might
> have had a proneness in respect to their vicinity, but I
> never took the time. I made my own living since I was
> fourteen and never seemed to get my ratiocinations
> equipped with the sentiments usually depicted toward
> the sect. I sometimes wish I had."

Advice to a love lorn son:

> "burn a few punk sticks in the hoss house to the great
> God Mazuma"

A burglar's resume:

> "The police, like yourself, scratch heads if they try to
> clarify me. No matter what you may think I am the
> respectable, humility prone burglar who is not above or

below his station. No masks, no dark lanterns, no gum shoes. Just a 38 in a pocket and peppermint gum."

Taking no chances:

"But this is going to be painless, ha, IF you raise both your hands above your head."
(The man raises his right hand)
"Up with the other one. You might be amphibious and shoot with your left."

I hope these adaptations of his tales for the stage provide another venue to preserve this irrepressible writer's artistry center stage for generations to come.

THE PERFECT FOOL

a one-act play based on THE RANSOM
OF MACK, a short story by O. Henry

SYNOPSIS

A man who thinks he has all the answers
jumps to a hasty and costly conclusion.

CHARACTERS

MACK	early forties, wise, gentle demeanor, self-effacing
ANDY	twenties, overly sure of himself, good guy
REBOSA REED	late teens, pretty, sexy, gaudy dresser

TIME	the early 1900s
SETTING	a small town thirty miles from Denver

The action of the play takes place on a
minimally set stage. A rocking chair and
other miscellaneous properties indicate
the interior of Mack and Andy's cottage as
necessary. Other action takes place in the
imaginary outdoors, on a road, etc.

As lights come up, Andy walks onto stage
carrying a small, well worn leather suitcase.
He stops center stage, puts suitcase down,
and addresses the audience. He wears an old
tweed suit, carries the jacket over his free
arm.

ANDY

This isn't where the story begins, but it is where the beginning of the end of the story began.

Everything else you might call prologue or prolusion.

See, I had received a telegram from Speight, the man that was working a mine I had an interest in out in New Mexico. I had to get out there and I was gone two months. I was anxious to get back to the little town of Pina and the two room cabin I shared with my friend Old Mack Lonsbury and enjoy life once more.

But two events shattered any hope of that.

As I approached the humble abode I shared with Old Mack...

> Rebosa Reed runs on stage, giggling, ignores Andy, stops, looks back off stage, giggles some more and exits other side of stage, still giggling. Rebosa's attire is on the gaudy side, tight fitting showing her very nice body. Her hat is large and decorated to overfull with pansies.

That was event number one!!

Event number two has to do with Old Mack himself. Now I say "old" but Mack wasn't really old, he was forty-one, but he always seemed old, quiet, thoughtful, wise... but sometimes as a body ages the mind recogitates its youth, and sometimes the mind gets stuck in that recogitation and thinks it IS youth! And that's why we got the saying "there's no fool like an old fool."

Anyway, here's a good place for that prolusion I mentioned, and that will bring us right back to the event number two, event number one you will remember was the high strung young lady running that-away full of some high spirited secret looked like to me.

> Lights start to dim

ANDY

Now me and old Mack, we got out of that Little Hide and Seek gold mine affair with about $40,000 apiece.

> Andy starts to walk backwards, suitcase in hand, as Mack enters, also suitcase in hand, and walking in place until Andy is side to side with him and also walking in place. They stop. Mack wears old style overalls and a loose fitting jacket.

> Lights to full.

MACK

Andy, I'm tired of hustling. You and me have been working hard together for three years. Say we knock off for awhile and spend some of this idle money we've coaxed our way.

ANDY

The proposition hits me just right. Let's be nabobs[1] for awhile and see how it feels. What'll we do, take in the Niagara Falls or buck at faro?[2]

MACK

For a good many years, I've thought that if I ever had extravagant money I'd rent a two-room cabin somewhere, hire us a cook and sit in my stocking feet and read Buckle's *History of Civilization*.[3]

ANDY

That sounds self-indulgent and gratifying without vulgar ostentation. And I don't see how money could be better invested. Give me a cuckoo clock and a Sep Winner's Self-Instructor for the banjo[4], and I'll join you.

MACK

Well look at that sign there. We are about to enter a town called Pina. Denver, it says, is thirty miles thataway.

ANDY

(reading the sign) Pop 340.

MACK

Sounds friendly enough for me. (looking at sign, he notices something, squints eyes, crouches a bit forward for a better look) Why look at that, that little sign underneath, hanging like an anecdote. See what it says?

ANDY

"Elegant two room house for rent." I think they saw us coming.

> Lights dim. In the semi darkness, actors
> leave suitcases off, move a rocking chair
> and an easy chair onto stage, and hang
> an outlandish cuckoo clock from a wire.
> (the cuckoo clock is optional, but if there
> is none, there can still be the sound effect.)
> Mack removes his clothes down to loose
> fitting long johns and blue yarn socks. Andy
> removes his jacket and brings a banjo onto
> stage. Mack sits in rocker with a thick book.
> Andy sits in easy chair and starts plucking
> the banjo. They both light up pipes. After
> a short pause the cuckoo sings out, once,
> raucously.

MACK

(closing his book as if on cue) If that isn't the darndest thing. Just when it gets too dark to read that darnded bird lets you know it.

ANDY

A nocturnal varmint it is. Diurnal too, seeing how it croaks when the sun comes up. Actually, the mechanism is so thin with age it's become time sensitive. Kinda like people, don't you think?

The men look at each other with blank
expressions. After a pause Andy speaks.

ANDY

It's your turn.

MACK

Mine. You sure? Let's see. Science... that was you. Pearl
diving, me. Sciatica, you. Egypt, me. Spelling, you. Fish, me.
Tradewinds, you. Leather, me. Gratitude, you, Eagles, me.

ANDY

A slight error. Fish AND Tradewinds, you. That made Leather,
me, Gratitude, you. Eagles, me. Your turn to pick the subject for
discussion.

There is a pause.

MACK

Hmmm, well.

As Mack ruminates, lights dim a bit.

Andy steps out of the scene and talks to the
audience.

ANDY

Now, listen closely, because the subject old Mack is about to
broach is intimately connected to(holds up one finger) the first
event, which you may remember was the young pretty thing
giggling that-away, and prologue to (holds up a second finger)
the second event, which is yet to come. And this on the very eve
of the day I am going to New Mexico for two months.

He re-enters the scene and sits as before.
Lights full.

MACK

Andy, friend, are you much apprised in the habits and policies of
women folks?

ANDY

Women?

MACK

You heard. Women.

ANDY

Why, yes. I know 'em from Alfred to Omaha. The feminine
nature and similitude is as plain to my sight as the Rocky
Mountains is to a blue-eye burro. I'm onto all their little
sidesteps and punctual discrepancies.

MACK

I tell you Andy (he sighs) I never had the least amount of
intersection with their predispositions. Maybe I might have had
a proneness in respect to their vicinity, but I never took the time.
I made my own living since I was fourteen and I never seemed
to get my ratiocinations equipped with the sentiments usually
depicted toward the sect. I sometimes wish I had.

Andy glances at Mack surreptitiously.

ANDY

Hmm. They're an adverse study and adapted to points of view.
Although they vary in rationale, I have found 'em quite often
obviously differing from each other in divergences of contrast.

MACK

It seems to me that a man had better take 'em in and secure his
inspirations of the sect when he's young and so preordained. I
let my chance go by; and I guess I'm too old now to go hopping
into the curriculum.

ANDY

Oh, I don't know. Maybe you better credit yourself with a
barrel of money and a lot of emancipation from a quantity of

uncontent. Still, I don't regret my knowledge of 'em. It takes a man who understands the symptoms and by-plays of women-folks to take care of himself in this world.

MACK

Hmm, I suppose. (gets up tiredly) Time to turn in. You have a good trip tomorrow to New Mexico.

> He exits. Lights dim. Andy exits, and then re-enters exactly as he did at the opening wearing his jacket and carrying his suitcase.

> Lights up. He stops centerstage and addresses the audience.

ANDY

Prolusion is now over. And here, again, comes the first event that shattered my hopes of a happy homecoming.

> Rebosa Reed runs across the stage giggling just as she did but this time she stops at far edge of stage and freezes.

> Lights up on rocking chair and easy chair and cuckoo. The place is empty... Andy walks to it, looks around.

ANDY

Mack... MACK!

> BRIGHT spot on Mack who enters sheepishly. Andy does a double. Mack is dressed elegantly as if for a dress ball (see description that Andy gives.)

MACK

Hello Andy. Glad to see you back. Things have happened since you went away.

ANDY

You're telling me! You are a spectacle. An undertaker's coat,
shiny shoes, (walks around Mack, looks under coat) a white
vest. A high silk hat! and what's this (indicates flower Mack has
pinned to his jacket), a geranium as big as an order of spinach.
And look at you, smirking and warping your face like an
infernal storekeeper or a kid with colic.

MACK

Like I said, things have happened since you went away.

ANDY

Happened, HAPPENED! Why I nearly fainted when I saw you.
If angels ever wept, I see no reason why they should be smiling
now. You are a sacrilegious sight, you are. God never made you
this way Mack Lonsbury. Why do you scarify his works with
this presumptious kind of ribaldry?

MACK

Why Andy, they've elected me justice of the peace since you left.

> Andy studies Mack closely. Mack is smiling
> and spirited.

ANDY

A justice of the peace ought to be disconsolate and assuaged.

> Rebosa giggles and jiggles, turns to the men,
> giggles some more.

ANDY

(to Mack) You are restless and (looks at Rebosa) and, inspired.

> Rebosa giggles some more. Mack raises his
> hat to her and bows. Rebosa curtsies, giggles
> and exits.

ANDY

Mack, Mack. (shakes his head) No hope for you if you've got the Mary-Jane infirmity at your age. I thought it wasn't going to take on you. And patent leather shoes? All this in two little short months!"

MACK

(in a kind of flutter) Tonight, I'm going to marry the young lady who just passed by.

> Andy slams his suitcase into Mack's arms.

ANDY

I forgot something at the post-office.

> He starts to exit as light go down. As lights come up, Rebosa enters from other side of stage followed shortly by Andy.

ANDY

AaaHEM.

> Rebosa stops, a bit in the style of old melodrama acting. She turns to Andy, overly innocent.

REBOSA

Yes. (she folds her hands, lowers her head demurely)

ANDY

Cut the blushing. This ain't a scene from the Two Orphans.[5]

> Rebosa shrugs, more her true self

ANDY

I understand you are to be married tonight.

REBOSA

Correct. You got any objections?

ANDY

Listen, sissy…

REBOSA

(in a pained tone) My name is Miss Rebosa Reed

ANDY

I know it. Now, Rebosa, I'm old enough to have owed money to your father. And that old, specious, dressed-up garbled, sea-sick ptomaine prancing around avidiously like an irremediable turkey gobbler with patent leather shoes on is my best friend. Why did you go and get him invested in this marriage business?

REBOSA

Why he was the only chance there was.

ANDY

Nay. Any man would admire your complexion and style of features. With your beauty you might pick any kind of a man. Listen, Rebosa. Old Mack ain't the man you want. He was twenty-two when you was nee Reed, as the papers say. This bursting into bloom won't last with him. He's all ventilated with oldness and rectitude and decay. Old Mack's down with a case of Indian summer. He overlooked his bet when he was young; and now he's suing Nature for the interest on the promissory note he took from Cupid instead of the cash. Rebosa are you bent on having this marriage occur?

REBOSA

Why sure I am. (she tosses her head so that the pansies on her hat oscillate) and so is somebody else I reckon.

ANDY

What time is it to take place?

REBOSA

At six o'clock.

ANDY

Rebosa, (he gets very charming) ain't there a young man in Pina, a nice young man that you think a heap of?

REBOSA

Yep. (nods her pansies) Sure there is! What do you think! Gracious!

ANDY

Does he like you? How does he stand in the matter?

REBOSA

Crazy. Ma has to wet down the front steps to keep him from sitting there all the time. But I guess that'll be all over after tonight. (she sighs)

ANDY

Rebosa, you don't really experience any of this adoration called love for old Mack, do you?

REBOSA

Lord! No. I think he's as dry as a lava bed. The idea!

ANDY

Who is this young man that you like, Rebosa?

REBOSA

It's Eddie Bayles. He clerks in Crosby's grocery. But he don't make but thirty-five a month. Ella Noakes was wild about him once.

ANDY

Old Mack tells me that his going to marry you at six o'clock this evening.

REBOSA

That's the time. It's to be at our house.

ANDY

Rebosa, listen to me. If Eddie Bayles had a thousand dollars cash—a thousand dollars mind you would buy him a store of his own—if you and Eddie had that much to excuse matrimony on would you consent to marry him this evening at FIVE o'clock?

> Rebosa stares at Andy for a minute, her expression blank.

ANDY

Now, Rebosa, I'm fully qualified to be an expert on the feminine mind. I can see those inadudible cogitations going on inside on you. Just answer the question.

REBOSA

A thousand dollars? Of course I would.

ANDY

Come on then, we'll go and see Eddie at Crosby's store. And then we'll go over to the bank and have our agreement witnessed by Mr. Porter, the president. Ah, you can read and write.

REBOSA

(personally humiliated) I am a sufferagette. (suffragette)

> He starts to move. Rebosa puts her hands out "halt"

REBOSA

At five o'clock? for a thousand dollars? Please don't wake me up. (she fans her face with her hands) Well, you ARE the rich uncle retired from the spice business in India.

> They start to exit. Rebosa stops, and puts her arm into Andy's.

REBOSA
You will be there? at the ceremony?

ANDY
Welllll, Rebosa, I'll give you my blessing right now. I got a date to go sit on a log and make cogitations on life and old age and the zodiac, and the ways of we humans, and all the disorder that goes with a lifetime, and how to disinvolve friends from relapses due to Indian Summer urging. And I'm going to give silent thanks that I have made a study of wom... that is, mankind, and cannot be deceived any by their means of conceit and evolution.

> He stares at her very satisfied with himself. She stares back. Lights down.

> Lights up. Mack in his old clothes, with his blue socks, sits in a rocker reading from the thick book.

> Andy enters, a study in nonchalance. Mack closes the book.

MACK
Hello Andy.

> He rocks. Andy paces.

ANDY
This don't look like getting ready for a wedding at six.

MACK
Oh, that was postponed.

ANDY
Postponed? just, postponed!

MACK

Just postponed.

Andy paces feverishly.

ANDY

Postponed until when?

MACK

Postponed back, to five o'clock, from six? They sent me a note saying the hour had been changed. It's all over now. It's a good thing I was dressed for the occasion early on. What made you stay away so long, Andy?

ANDY

"They" sent you a note. (pauses) So, you heard about the wedding!?

MACK

I was there! I operated it. I told you I was justice of the peace. The preacher is off East to visit his folks, and I'm the only one in town to perform the dispensations of marriage. I promised Eddie and Rebosa a month ago I'd marry 'em.

Andy sits, stupefied, the truth of the situation sinking in.

ANDY

One thousand dollars.

MACK

Hmmm?

ANDY

One thousand dollars.

MACK

Oh so you heard about Rebosa getting that mysterious inheritance. Some rich uncle, retired from the spice trade in India. And guess what. Eddie and Rebosa are going to buy the store from old man Crosby. My, my. (he touches his cheek) She gave me the nicest kiss, and she smelled so sweet and perfumey. She said the scent was Sunshine and Roses. And she said, "I am so glad the priest was away and that YOU were my only chance I had, because, you are my good luck charm." My, my. Ain't life, just... so... perfect sometimes.

A silence.

MACK

Your turn. To choose the subject for discussion.

ANDY

Fools.

MACK

Fools?

ANDY

The darndest fools, the biggest fool, the, the... (shakes his fist searching for words)

MACK

How about the perfect fool. Hmmm. I'd say that is someone who jumps to conclusions fomented by a specious highly-developed sense of knowing everything about a subject that can't ever be fully and thoroughly known about.

Pause. As lights dim the cuckoo sings out.

END OF PLAY.

THE PERFECT STRANGER

a one-act play based on MAKES THE
WHOLE WORLD KIN, a short story by
O. Henry

SYNOPSIS

A burglar and his victim find they have
something in common.

CHARACTERS

MAN   middle-aged man

BURGLAR   middle-aged man

TIME   The early 1900s.

SETTING   The man's bedroom in his mansion. The
action of the play can take place on a
minimal set; the walls are suggested with
simple framing with a suggestion of a door
on one side (door may be practical if desired)
There is a bed, a dresser with odds and ends
on it—crumpled roll of money, a watch,
keys, a small stack of poker chips, crushed
cigars in a tray, a pink silk hair bow and a
bottle of bromo-seltzer.

The stage is lit by a gas lamp turned low.

The Man, wearing pajamas, sleeps in the
bed. Quietly the burglar appears at the door,
as he slowly opens it half way.

He wears a blue sweater and casual trousers
and regular shoes. He chews gum as he

thoughtfully peers in. The man in the bed murmurs and tosses. The burglar stays calm and holds his action until the man quiets and snores a bit. The burglar now steps into the room. He looks around and shakes his head in affirmation as if the room is just as he thought it would be.

The burglar takes a step toward the dresser. The man makes a squeaky groan. The burglar, remaining totally unperturbed stops. The man groans slightly then quiets. The burglar crosses to the dresser quietly and surveys the odds and ends. He picks up the tray holding the cigars and sniffs at them. He nods his head as if assessing the value of the cigars and nods approvingly. He puts the tray down and holds up the bromo-seltzer, nods knowingly as he touches his own stomach, looks at the sleeping man sympathetically, and puts the bromo-seltzer down. He picks up the hair bow gingerly between two fingers and holds it out in front of him and examines it. He puts it down. He reaches for the money knocking over the stack of poker chips. This creates a metallic sound.

On cue the man wakens with a small gasp, his right hand sliding under his pillow but remaining there as simultaneously the burglar pulls out a .38-calibre revolver from his pocket and points it at the man. They stare at each other. The burglar chews his gum calmly.

BURGLAR

(in a conversational tone) Lay still.

MAN

(looks around, mystified) How'd you?....

BURGLAR

...get in?

MAN

Yes.

BURGLAR

I took my time.

MAN

Excuse me.

BURGLAR

Anyone who respects his profession or his Art takes their time,
before they take anything else. You understand?

MAN

I, (he starts to move, the burglar makes a motion with his gun
to "stop" and the man lies back) I'm not sure I understand.

BURGLAR

You ever see the artistes with their canvases on the street side
painting a church, or a statue? What do they do? They "look"
at the subject. Realllly look. I too am an artiste. I looked at
this house of yours. A private residence. Boarded front door.
Untrimmed "Boston" ivy. Sure signs that the mistress of the
house is sitting on some oceanside piazza telling a sympathetic
man, (The man stirs. The burglar waves the gun. The man stills)
telling a sympathetic man in a yachting cap that no one had ever
understood her sensitive, lonely heart. Furthermore, there were
no lighted windows except one.

MAN

This one.

BURGLAR

You catch on. Third-story, front. It's late in the day and in the season. September. Speaking of time, (he waves his gun) it's time for you to sit up and hold up both your hands.

> The man hestitates, glances quickly towards his right hand, sits up. He has a little, pointed, brown-and-gray beard. The burglar leans closer and studies the man's face.

BURGLAR

Ha, for a minute there I thought you were my dentist. He has a little beard, going gray, pointing down from his chin like an arrow. And, he looks solid, esteemed, and irritable and disgusted. Just like you right now. But, this is going to be "painless", ha, IF, you raise both your hands above your head.

> The man hestitates. The Burglar waves the gun. The man raises his right hand.

BURGLAR

Up with the other one. You might be amphibious and shoot with your left. You can count two, can't you? Hurry up, now.

> The man doesn't move. The Burglar chews his gum. He makes a small threatening step towards the bed.

MAN

Can't raise the other one.

> He moves his left shoulder slightly and winces.

BURGLAR

What's the matter with it?

MAN

Rheumatism in the shoulder.

BURGLAR

Inflammatory?

MAN

Was. The inflammation has gone down

> The burglar stands for a moment or two
> holding his gun on the man. He glances
> at the money on the dresser and then,
> half-embarrassed, looks back to the man.
> Suddenly, the burglar makes a grimace as if
> in pain.

MAN

Don't stand there making faces. If you've come to burgle why
don't you do it? There's some stuff lying around. Artist indeed.
Scoundrel more like it. Spying on a honest man's activity as if he
were an insect you can step on. Let me give you some advice It
is autumn of the year, and judging your age to be close to mine,
it is the autumn of the soul. I have come to see roof gardens
and stenographers as vanities. I wish my mate would too for I
desire a return to what is durable; the blessings of decorum and
the moral excellencies. And you should come to that realization
too. Now take your plunder and go. Or do your worst and
pull the trigger of that thing that looks like some monstrous
growth upon your body. (the burglar is silent) Well? (the burglar
remains silent) Damn. (he pounds the bed with his right arm.)

> The BURGLAR waves the pistol, the man
> raises his right arm

BURGLAR

Hmmm. (looks at the gun) Monstrous growth.

MAN

(after a pause) Where did you get in?

BURGLAR
Window. Ground floor, library. Lock is loose. It's a lock shaped
like a comma that fits in under the lip of the other half. A little
vibration towards the inside and the comma slides out of the lip.

MAN
So you've been through the entire house. You saw that our
furniture is swathed in its summer dust protectors. The silver is
far away in safe-deposit vaults. What kind of a devilish "haul"
did you expect? If you surmised the woman of the house was
away, could you not then deduce the only "touch" you might
make was some loose money here or there, or did your artistic
eye fail to reveal the simplicity of my daily regime? Some artist
you are. You see me as rich in worldly goods and assume the
pickings will be plentiful and easy to make, like fruit fallen from
an overripe tree. But the real me is nothing like your picture of
me. My advice to you is: never become a real artist.

Your paintings would be horrible to see. Why look at you.
You don't even LOOK like a burglar.

BURGLAR
I belong to the third type of burglars, can't you tell.

MAN
What? Third type?

BURGLAR
The police and the writers of detective books have made us
familiar with the first and second type. Their classification is
simple. I will quote from memory (clears his throat, interrupts
himself) not one hundred percent but of what I seen in the
policeman's handbook and of which I have read in the mystery
volumes. I here now give you the gist. (clears his throat again
and speaks as if reciting) The collar is the distinguishing mark.
When a burglar is caught who does not wear a collar he is
described as a degenerate of the lowest type, singularly vicious
and depraved. He is suspected of being the desperate criminal
who stole the handcuffs out of Patrolman Hennessy's pocket in

1878 and walked away to escape arrest. The other well-known type is the burglar who wears a collar. He is always referred to as a Raffles in real life. He is invariably a gentlemen by daylight, breakfasting in a dress suit, and posing as a paperhanger, while after dark he plies his nefarious occupation. His mother is an extremely wealthy and respected resident of Ocean Grove and when he is conducted to his cell he asks at once for a nail file and the Police Gazette. He always has a wife in every State of the Union and fiancees in all the Territories and the newspapers print his matrimonial gallery out of their stock of cuts of the ladies who were cured by only one bottle after having been given up by five doctors, experiencing great relief after the first dose. (stops reciting)I am neither Raffles nor one of the chefs from Hell's Kitchen. The police, like yourself, scratch heads if they try to clarify me. No matter what you may think I am the respectable, humility prone burglar who is not above or below his station. No masks, no dark lanterns, no gumshoes.[1] Just a .38 in a pocket and peppermint gum. Want some? (he winces quietly with pain)

                    MAN
What's the matter with you?

                    BURGLAR
'Scuse me, it just socked me one too. Right there in the shoulder. It's good for you that rheumatism and me happens to old pals. I got it in my left arm too. Most anybody but me would have popped you when you wouldn't hoist that left claw of yours.

                    MAN
How long have you had it?

                    BURGLAR
Four years. I guess that ain't all. Once you've got it, it's you for a rheumatic life—that's my judgment.

> They are silent. The burglar lowers the gun,
> thinks about it, raises it slowly, then lowers
> it again.

MAN

Ever try rattlesnake oil?

BURGLAR

Gallons. If all the snakes I've used the oil of was strung out in
a row they'd reach eight times as far as Saturn, and the rattle
could be heard at Valparaiso, Indiana and back.

MAN

Some use Chiselum's Pills.

BURGLAR

Fudge? Took 'em five months. No good. I had some relief the
year I tried Finkelham's Extract, Balm of Gilead poultices, and
Pott's Pain Pulverizer; but I think it was the buckeye I carried in
my pocket what done the trick.

MAN

Is yours worse in the morning or at night?

BURGLAR

Night. Just when I'm busiest. Say, take down that arm of
yours—I guess you won't—Say! did you ever try Blickerstaff's
Blood Builder?(the man lowers his arm)

MAN

I never did. Does yours come in paroxysms or is it a steady pain?

> The burglar sits on the foot of the bed and
> rests his gun on his crossed knee.

BURGLAR

It jumps. It strikes me when I ain't looking for it. I had to give
up second-story work because I got stuck sometimes half-way
up. Tell you what—I don't believe the bloomin' doctors know
what is good for it.

MAN

Same here. I've spent a thousand dollars without getting any relief. Yours swell any?

BURGLAR

Of mornings. And when it's goin to rain—great Christopher!

MAN

Me, too. I can tell when a streak of humidity the size of a tablecloth starts from Florida on its way to New York. And if I pass a theater where there's an *East Lynne* [2] matinee going on, the moisture starts my left arm jumping like a toothache.

BURGLAR

It's undiluted – hades!

MAN

You're dead right.

> The burglar looks down at his pistol, shrugs, puts the pistol into a pocket, awkwardly trying to be at ease.

BURGLAR

Say, old man, ever try opodeldoc? [3]

MAN

Stop! Might as well rub on restaurant butter.

BURGLAR

Sure. It's a salve suitable for little Minnie when the kitty scratches her finger. I'll tell you what! We're up against it. I only find one thing that eases her up. Hey? Little old sanitary, ameliorating, lest-we-forget Booze. Say—this job's off—'scuse me—get on your clothes and let's go out and have some. 'Scuse the liberty, but—ouch! There she goes again!

MAN

For a week, I haven't been able to dress myself without help. I'm afraid, ah, Thomas is in...

BURGLAR

That his name. I know. He's in bed. Sound.

MAN

Yes, well…he's in bed and…

BURGLAR

Climb out. I'll help you get into your duds.

> There is an awkwardness and shyness. The
> man strokes his beard.

MAN

It's very unusual….

> The burglar takes a shirt from the back of
> the chair.

BURGLAR

Here's your shirt. Fall out.

> The man slowly gets out of bed.

MAN

Are you sure?

BURGLAR

Sure I'm sure.

> He helps the man out of the top of the
> pajamas. He reaches for the tie on the
> bottoms but the man reacts to stop him. The
> burglar helps the man into his shirt.

MAN

My trousers are…are you sure?

BURGLAR

Sure. Where are they?

MAN

Under my pillow.

> The burglar retrieves the trousers from under
> the pillows of the bed where they were laid
> out neatly.

BURGLAR

Pressed while you sleep. (he reaches under the pillows again holds up a revolver) Hmmm. Some iron. (He lays the revolver on the bed)

MAN

For an emergency, you know. Course with the rheumatism.

> He shrugs, turns his back to the burglar.
> As he steps out of the pajama bottoms, he
> topples a bit and has to lean on the burglar's
> shoulder. Both are shy, the man doing his
> best to perform the task unassisted and
> the burglar awkwardly helping where he
> can. The man buttons the top button of his
> trousers. They stare at each other.

BURGLAR

Shall we (He indicates the door. The man starts to cross) I know a man who said Omberry's Ointment fixed him in two weeks so he could use both hands in tying his four-in-hand. (The man stops)

MAN

Liked to forgot my money. Laid it on the dresser.

> As he crosses past the burglar, the burglar
> catches him by the right arm.

BURGLAR

Come on. I asked you. Leave it alone. I've got the price.

The man looks at the burglar. The burglar nods, points to the door. The man starts to cross followed by the burglar.

BURGLAR
Ever try witch hazel and oil of wintergreen?

They freeze.

Lights down.

END OF PLAY.

THE PERFECT ARCHER

a one-act play based on MAMMON AND
THE ARCHER, a short story by O. Henry

SYNOPSIS

A wealthy man thinks money can buy
anything, including the time his son needs
to ask the girl he loves to marry him. And
he seems to succeed. Or was it really Cupid
who arranged it?

CHARACTERS

ANTHONY ROCKWALL	fifties, strong personality, good man
ELLEN	his sister, sixties, refined, gentle
RICHARD	his son, twenties, good looking, earnest
EVELYN	RICHARD's girlfriend, twenties, pretty, spirited
ALICE	maid to ROCKWALL, thirties, lovable
KELLY	ROCKWALL's handyman, thirties, smooth operator, mischievous
TIME	The early 1900s
SETTING	ROCKWALL's opulently furnished library in his Fifth Avenue mansion

Scene One   Early evening

Scene Two   Later that same night

SCENE ONE

As the CURTAIN RISES, ROCKWALL stands upstage, looking out a window at the street below. He chews on a cigar. Sitting on one of the easy chairs is ELLEN, embroidery in hand. ROCKWALL chuckles, pats his stomach in contentment.

ROCKWALL

Ha...HA...HAAA...he sees it...he SEES it!

ELLEN

How can he not? Your next door neighbor would have to be blind not to. You keep adding and adding to your replicas of Italian renaissance sculpture. Soon you will have to have this ostentatious house of yours moved backwards to accommodate your front yard which is rapidly becoming overfull with replicas of European statuary.

ROCKWALL

He's European, ain't he? G. Van Schuylight Suffolk-Jones. He should feel right at home. Ha...HAAA! (He watches) There he goes to his motorcar...AHA...one more look of contempt our way, wrinkling a contumelious nostril.

ELLEN

I can't say as I blame him or your neighbor on the other side of this "Soap" palace you have erected between them. This was a genteel neighborhood of tasteful architecture.

ROCKWALL

Genteel! The only difference between me and Suffolk-Jones is that he inherited his fortune, while I made my own. (He leans toward the window and raises his voice) The Eden Musee'll[1] get the old frozen Nesselrode[2] yet if you don't watch out! Ha! (He turns away form the window) I'll have this house painted red, white and blue and see if that'll make his Dutch nose turn up any higher.

ELLEN
Dear brother. (She sighs)

If I didn't know that under that gruff exterior there beats a heart of gold, I would despair. Truly I would. And speaking of hearts, there is a member of this household who is nursing a broken one. Or haven't you noticed?

ROCKWALL
Rubbish...broken heart. (He takes a wad of money from a pocket) The best broken-heart preventative in the world. And there's more coming! (He waves the money) DETERGENT... perfumed laundry lotion...why it could be as big as my original Eureka Soap! (He goes to the desk and flips through papers) Hmmm...hmmmmm...what was his name?

ELLEN
James Dillingham Young, the perfumer. His Lilac Embrace and Sunshine and Roses are very popular now.

ROCKWALL
Precisely. James Dillingham Young ah, yes. I must call on him tomorrow to see what scent he has composed for... (He pauses, strikes an oratorical pose) Eureka Detergent! DETER. Ha, I like that word. Hold off, hold "dirt" in suspension. Here! (He strikes another oratorical pose) MAKE YOUR LINENS A VERITABLE GARDEN. What do you think, sister mine? What do you think of that?

ELLEN
(Politely stifling a yawn) Well, gardens, unlike linens, need dirt, do they not?

ROCKWALL
Hmmm. I see, yes. I'll have to think of something else.

ELLEN
Right now, think of someBODY else.

ROCKWALL

Hmmm. That, yes. (He calls loudly) ALICE...ALICE, you, you... (He can't think of what else to call her) ...you maid, you. Leave the brandy alone and get in here. (He waits, paces) When I was an employee, I ran. RAN!, when I was called. Now they... (He imitates someone walking very slowly)

> ALICE enters slowly, unperturbed. She stops, hands on hips.

ALICE

You rang?

ROCKWALL

I. HUH? NOOO. I did not "rang." I never cared for bells. I heard too many of them when I was a grunt employee in the salt mines. Bells and whistles! And I will not have a rope in every one of my rooms to be pulled so a bell announces to my employees that I request their attendance, genteeeel though that may be. (ELLEN and ALICE exchange knowing glances)

ROCKWALL

I have a perfectly sound pair of lungs, vocal chords, tongue, teeth and lips to form the sound I care to expel with sufficient volume to penetrate every last corner of this house.

ALICE

(After a bit of a pause) What was that you said, Sir?

ELLEN

Has Richard left the house yet?

ALICE

Not yet, Ma'am.

ELLEN

Tell him, please, that his father wishes to see him.

ALICE

Right away, ma'am. Will that be all ma'am…er, I mean, Sir?
(ROCKWALL stares at her, turns away. ALICE curtsies and
exits.)

ROCKWALL

(Turning to ELLEN) Corruption. You have corrupted the
employer-employee relationship.

> He rumples his hair with one hand and
> rattles the keys in his pocket with the other.
> He grabs a newspaper and sits in the other
> easy chair, rustling the paper as he opens it.
>
> RICHARD enters. He is dressed for the
> theater, but his demeanor is forlorn. He
> crosses to ELLEN and kisses her on the
> top of her head. ELLEN pats his arm.
> RICHARD starts to walk to his father,
> stops shyly. ROCKWALL waves an
> agitated, self-conscious wave at RICHARD,
> and RICHARD backs off slightly, also
> self-conscious.

ROCKWALL

Richard, my boy, what do you pay for the soap that you use?
(RICHARD looks to ELLEN) Come, come. I know you don't
use Eureka. It's the plumber whose house doesn't have the latest
plumbing.

ELLEN

My dear brother, you are as full of unexpectedness as a girl at
her first party. Richard is only six months home from college
and perhaps has not yet re-acclimated himself to your measure.

ROCKWALL

And what, dear sister, does that mean? That college made him
genteeeel? (He looks at Richard) Well? How much do you pay
for the soap that you use?

RICHARD

Six dollars a dozen, I think, Dad.

ROCKWALL

And your clothes?

RICHARD

I suppose about sixty dollars, as a rule.

ROCKWALL

Then you ARE a gentleman! I've heard of these young bloods
spending $24 a dozen for soap and going over the hundred mark
for clothes. You've got as much money to waste as any of 'em,
and yet you stick to what's decent and moderate. Now I use the
Old Eureka. Not only for sentiment, but it's the purest soap
made. Whenever you pay more than 10 cents a cake for soap,
you buy bad perfumes and labels. But 50 cents is doing very well
for a young man in your generation, position and condition. As
I said, you're a gentleman. They say it takes three generations
to make one. But THEY are off. Money'll do it as slick as soap
grease. It's made you one. By Hokey! It's almost made one of me.

ELLEN coughs

ROCKWALL

I'm nearly as impolite and disagreeable and ill mannered as
those two old knickerbockers gents on each side of me that can't
sleep of nights because I bought and built in between 'em.

RICHARD

(Gloomily) Well…

ROCKWALL

Yes?

RICHARD

There are some things that money can't accomplish.

ROCKWALL

NOW, DON'T SAY THAT. I am shocked! I bet my money on
money every time. I've been through the encyclopedia down to
Y looking for something you can't buy with it and I expect to
have to take up the appendix next week. I'm for money against
the field. Tell me something money won't buy.

RICHARD

(Slightly rankled) For one thing, it won't buy into the exclusive
circles of society. Will it, Aunt Ellen?

ROCKWALL

Oho! Won't it? (He rises and thunders at them) OHO, WON'T
IT! You tell me where your exclusive circles would be if the first
Astor hadn't had the money to pay for his steerage passage over!

ELLEN

Money is the root of evil. And the way you thunder, you are its
champion. Now stop putting off what it is you want to talk to
Richard about.

ROCKWALL

(Calming down) And that's what I was coming to. That's why I
asked you to come in. I... (He paces)

RICHARD

Yes, Dad?

ROCKWALL

(He looks at ELLEN. SHE gets busier with her sewing.) There's
something going wrong with you, boy. I've been noticing it
for some time. (He looks at ELLEN. SHE stares back at him
innocently. HE turns to Richard.) Out with it. I guess I could
lay my hands on eleven millions within twenty-four hours,
besides the real estate. If it's your liver, there's the Rambler down
in the bay, coaled and ready to steam down to the Bahamas in
two days.

RICHARD

Not a bad guess, Dad. You haven't missed it far. It's not my liver, it's...

ROCKWALL

Of course not...hmmm... (He looks at ELLEN. SHE points to her heart.) Huh... ah... ahhhh... heart... Ahaaa...what's her name? (RICHARD hesitates, looks from ELLEN to his father.) Come on, boy. Crude though I may be, you're confidence won't be betrayed, unless... (He points to ELLEN)

RICHARD

Oh, Aunt Ellen already knows. (Pauses. Then, as if dreaming) Evelyn Lantry.

ROCKWALL

Lantry. Lantry...

ELLEN

Lantry Publishing House. Some of those books you like. The Pirates and the Princess.

ROCKWALL

AHA, good. GOOD, my boy. Well, this isn't bad atall, not atall.

RICHARD

It's not?

ROCKWALL

Elementary, my boy. Why don't you just ask her? I demand that you just... ask her. You've got the money and the looks and you're a decent boy. Your hands are clean. You've got no Eureka soap on 'em. You've been to college, but she'll overlook that.

RICHARD

I haven't had a chance to ask her.

ROCKWALL

Make one. Take her for a walk in the park or a straw ride, or walk home with her from church. Chance! Pshaw! Write a note!

RICHARD

You don't know the social mill, Dad. She's part of the stream that turns it. Every hour and minute of her time is arranged for days in advance. (He crosses to his father)

I must have that girl, Dad, or this town is a blackjack swamp forevermore. And I can't write it. I can't do that.

ROCKWALL

(Very sympathetic) Tut. tut. Do you mean to tell me that with all the money I've got, you can't get an hour or two of a girl's time to yourself?

ELLEN

Money, money. This is an affair of the heart, my brother dear.

RICHARD

I've put it off too late. She's going to sail for Europe at noon day after tomorrow for two years' stay. I'm to see her alone this evening for a few minutes. She's at Larchmont now at her aunt's. I can't go there, but I'm allowed to meet her with a cab at the Grand Central Station at the 8:30 train. We drive down Broadway to Wallack's at a gallop, where her mother and a box party will be waiting for us in the lobby. Do you think she would listen to a declaration from me during that six or eight minutes under those circumstances? No. And what chance would I have in the theater or afterward? None. No, Dad, this is one tangle that your money can't unravel. We can't buy one minute of time with cash. If we could, rich people would live longer. There's not hope of getting a talk with Miss Landry before she sails.

ROCKWALL

Hmmm. All right, Richard, my boy. Cheerful boy, stay cheerful, like your old man here. You run along now. Seems like you've got quite a fixed time schedule. I'm glad it ain't your liver. But don't forget to burn a punk stick in the joss house to the great god Mazuma[5] from time to time. You say money won't buy time? Well, of course you can't order eternity wrapped up and delivered at your residence for a price, but I've seen Father Time get pretty bad stone bruises on his heels when he walked through the gold diggings.

ELLEN

Richard, before you go, my darling. (She rises and takes a ring from her finger.)

Wear it tonight, dear nephew. Your mother gave it to me. She said it brought good luck in love. She asked me to give it to you when you had found the one you loved.

RICHARD

(He holds up the ring reverently) Mother's. Oh, Dad.

ROCKWALL

Thank you, Ellen. Put it on, son, put it on. (RICHARD tries the ring, but it won't fit.)

RICHARD

I'll put it in my vest pocket next to my heart.

> RICHARD kisses ELLEN on the forehead.
> SHE pats the pocket. HE starts to leave,
> turns to his father, starts for him, both men
> self-conscious.

ROCKWALL

Go, boy, go. They've got you timed to the second, it seems to me. Phone for that cab.

> RICHARD bows slightly and EXITS

ROCKWALL

(Goes to his desk and thumps on it) My total bank account at his service, and he begins to knock money. Says money couldn't help. Says the rules of society couldn't be bucked for a yard by a team of ten-millionaires. Hmmm…hmmmmm.

ELLEN

You control millions of dollars! Oh, Anthony, I wish you would not think so much of money. Wealth is nothing where a true affection is concerned. Love is all powerful. If he had only spoken earlier! She could not have refused our Richard. But now I fear it is too late. He will have no opportunity to address her. Your millions cannot control that. All your gold cannot bring happiness to your son.

ELLEN EXITS, sadly

ROCKWALL

ALICE...AAAALLLICE!

> ALICE enters, a bit flustered, as though she has been interrupted at some secret business. She hiccups and burps. ROCKWALL stares at her knowingly.

ROCKWALL

My best brandy, I presume.

ALICE

Why, no, sir, not your bes...Well, just a wee sip to correct what ails me.

ROCKWALL

Never mind, never mind. Where can I find Kelly?

ALICE

Him, sir. That common dog? Always sniffing at me skirts, he is. This girl ain't no common bone, so's how'd I know where he's likely to be?

ROCKWALL

Common is what made this country and, seems to me, you are commonly around when Kelly puts in an appearance in this house.

ALICE

'Tis me duty, sir, to see to it that scruff dolt wastes none of yer precious time. I keep my eye on him so you can avoid him when you want to and...

ROCKWALL

...AND when I want to FIND him. Well?

ALICE

He's, ahhhm. He's. Well, ya see, sir, there was a loose window in the wine cellar, and I took it upon myself, soon as I seen the mangy dog, to have him fix the latch, seein' how he's so handy with, ahhh, his hands.

ROCKWALL

Handy with his hands, huh, hmmm? So, get him, girl, get him! No, never mind. I'll do it myself. There's no time to waste. (He starts to exit, bellowing as he goes.) Kelly, you knave! You Irish hooligan! Come out of that wine cellar. KELLYYYYY!

END OF SCENE ONE

SCENE TWO

Hours later. ROCKWALL sits in an easy
chair reading a book. He wears a plush
red dressing gown. Slowly a commotion of
voices is heard offstage, the voices growing
louder as people approach the door to the
library. The voices are excited and happy.
ELLEN bursts in, followed by RICHARD
and EVELYN LANTRY, arm in arm,
followed by a tipsy ALICE.

ELLEN

Anthony, dear, dear, dear brother!

ROCKWALL stands, not quite knowing
what to expect.

ELLEN

A miracle, no less than a miracle.

ALICE

Ah, men… (She hiccups)

RICHARD

(Still arm in arm with EVELYN, HE completely,
unselfconsciously tugs at this father's arm.) Dad. Look. LOOK!
A dream come true, Dad. You are looking at a dream come true.
(He kisses EVELYN's hand) Evelyn, I present you to my father.

ROCKWALL

Whaaa? Evelyn Lantry? But the time schedule, the theater?
Every minute of the clock filled with this and that.

EVELYN

Gone forever. All I have time for now is to… (She almost
swoons into RICHARD's arms) …to gaze. Oh, how deep.
deep…

The YOUNG LOVERS swoon towards each other, lips puckered

ALICE

Ah...men (Hiccups)

RICHARD and EVELYN break away

RICHARD

What time is it?

EVELYN

Forget time.

RICHARD

But how long has it been since, life began. Let me see. At eight thirty-two, I captured you out of that gabbing mob at the station.

EVELYN

Oh. I tried so hard not to show my eagerness to escape. So I said, "We mustn't keep Mamma and the others waiting," and you said to the driver...

RICHARD

"To Wallacks' Theater[4] as fast as you can drive."

EVELYN

So loyal, to keep up the pretense.

RICHARD

What I really wanted to say was " I'M IN LOVE WITH PERFECTION!" No work of art can compare to the original masterpiece.

EVELYN

OHHH...Richard...

THEY steal a quick kiss.

ALICE

Oh, my heart will break!

> She starts to sob, sits in an easy chair,
> touching her skirt hem to her eyes.

ELLEN

See, dear brother. Affection unleashed.

ROCKWALL

But...still...how...what?

RICHARD

Oh, my poor *mon pere*. (to Evelyn) That's French.

EVELYN

The French are wicked.

> THEY giggle.

ALICE

So are the Irish. Those mangy dogs.

ELLEN

Tell your father. Tell him the entire miracle.

ROCKWALL

Oh, indeed. indeed.

RICHARD

We whirled up Forty-second to Broadway, and then down the white-starred lane that leads from the soft meadows of sunset to the rocky hills of morning.

ALICE

Ahhh, a poet he is from inside out. And the only men I have are, guttersnipes. (Blows her nose.)

EVELYN

But then, at Thirty-fourth, my, my KING Richard halted our dash to nowhere by quickly thrusting up the trap and, with a dominant tone, ordered the cabman to STOP! My hair curled at the back of my neck at this display of authority. THE Crusader had entered my life!

RICHARD

Both the driver and the horse were perturbed, he sighing, "What now?" and the spirited nag pawing the ground with impatience. "The world must wait," I said, "for I have dropped..." (He pauses) "...my mother's ring."

ELLEN and ALICE gasp

ELLEN and ALICE

Noooooo!

RICHARD

"I would hate to lose it. I won't detain you for a minute for, as it left the proximity to my heart, it was as if a silver beam directed my eye to where it fell."

ALICE

Boo hooooo. No more, no more! (She blows her nose.)

EVELYN

And in less than a minute. (She looks at RICHARD)

He was back in the cab with the ring, its many facets gleaming like stars.

ELLEN

And now, dear brother, listen well to the miracle.

All is quiet

ROCKWALL

I'm listening, but I don't hear anything.

RICHARD

Dad. Father. In that minute, that one minute. No, less, forty seconds?

EVELYN
Thirty, thirty-five.

ROCKWALL
Cutting it fine are we? The gist, dear boy, the gist.

RICHARD
In that brief time... (ALL wait) A CROSSTOWN CAR HAD
STOPPED DIRECTLY IN FRONT OF THE CAB! (he
acts it out now, grabbing Alice up and putting her and then
ELLEN in front of him.) The cabman tried to pass to the left,
but... (ALICE moves in) ...a heavy express wagon cut him off.
He tried to the right... (ELLEN moves in) ...and had to back
away from a furniture van that had no business to be there. He
tried to back out... (EVELYN blocks him) ...but dropped his
reins and swore dutifully. (He is now encircled by the THREE
WOMEN, who close in on him) We were blockaded in a
tangled mess of vehicles and horses.

EVELYN
(She breaks from the pack.) Still worried about Mamma, I cried
out, "Why don't you drive on? We'll be late!" (Pauses) But I
think. I think, I was hoping it was impossible to drive on.

RICHARD
I stood up in the cab. (ELLEN and ALICE fall back.
RICHARD stands on an easy chair.)

I looked around. I saw a congested flood of wagons, trucks,
cabs, vans and streetcars FILLING the vast space where
Broadway, Sixth Avenue and Thirty-Fourth Street cross one
another as a twenty-SIX inch maiden fills her twenty-TWO inch
girdle.

EVELYN
Richard... (She slaps at his legs playfully)

RICHARD

And still, from all the cross streets they were hurrying and
rattling themselves into the straggling mass, locking wheels
and adding their drivers' imprecations to the clamor. The entire
traffic of Manhattan seemed to have jammed itself around
them. I heard an old time New Yorker among the thousands
of spectators that lined the sidewalks shout out that he had not
witnessed a street blockade of the proportions of this one ever!!
(He gets down from the chair and takes Evelyn's hands.) "I'm
very sorry," I said. "It looks as if we are stuck. They won't get
this jumble loosened up in an hour. It was my fault. If I hadn't
dropped the ring, we…"

EVELYN

"Let me SEE the ring. Now that it can't be helped, I don't care.
I think theaters, right now, are stupid anyway, and so are time
schedules, and decorum that belies the aspirations of one's heart.
I will live in the shade, no longer being merely Evelyn Lantry. I
will come out into the light as Mrs. Richard Rockwall!"

> ALICE breaks down in a mass of tears and
> falls against ELLEN, who hugs her tenderly.

ELLEN

Alice, perhaps some fresh brewed coffee. And isn't there
some of your cheesecake still left over from dinner? Perhaps a
celebration.

EVELYN

Oh, Aunt Ellen. Let me help. I must fasten my energy onto
some task, or…or… (She hugs RICHARD, kisses him, then
turns to ROCKWALL, hugs him and kisses him on the cheek.)
Dad! (She whirls around, takes ALICE's hand) Come, Alice. Is
that brandy I detect? Lead me on.

> Laughing, EVELYN and ALICE EXIT

Silence. RICHARD shakes his head as if
still not believing it all.

RICHARD

I. All the stops have been pulled away for her, too. In an instant
we discovered who we really were. Oh, Dad, I hope you are
happy, too. (He takes his father's hand)

ROCKWALL

Mmmmmm…. (then expansively) Of course, my boy! (He
opens his arms, and RICHARD rushes in) Now, go help them.
We will have the coffee and cheesecake in here.

RICHARD EXITS

ROCKWALL picks up his book

ELLEN

(Seizes the book from him) OH, NO!

ROCKWALL

Sister, I've got my pirate there in that book in a devil of a scrape.
His ship has just been scuttled and he's too good a judge of
money to let it drown. I wish you would let me go on with this
chapter.

ELLEN

Money! They're engaged, Anthony. She has promised to marry
our Richard. On their way to the theater there was a street
blockade and it was two hours before the cab could get out of
it. And, oh, Brother Anthony, don't ever boast of the power
of money again. A little emblem of true love, a little ring that
symbolized unending and non mercenary affection was the
cause of our Richard finding his happiness. He dropped it in the
street… (She is reliving the story. ROCKWALL nods politely.)
…but a silver beam, the trajectory of love's arrow pointed to
where the treasure lay. And before they could continue, the
blockade occurred. Providence provided him the time so that he

could speak to his love. And win her! There, while the cab was hemmed in. Money is dross compared with true love, Anthony.

ROCKWALL
(Reaching for his book, which SHE hands to him) All right. I'm glad the boy has got what he wanted. I told him I wouldn't spare any expense in the matter if...

ELLEN
But what could your money have done? You couldn't buy him the time.

> There is a commotion offstage. ALICE
> rushes in followed by KELLY, who wears
> colorful attire with a blue polka-dot necktie.

ALICE
I told 'em this was no time to come botherin' ya, sir. But the bloodhound seems to be on some trail he won't let go of. He insisted he had to see ya.

ROCKWALL
Yes. It's all right, Alice. Help the children., off with you.

> ALICE glares at KELLY, who pinches here
> cheek. SHE yelps, slaps at him, and plows
> out of the room, head high.

KELLY
Come to settle the account, govna. Ah... (He nods his head in ELLEN's direction) ...she all right?

ELLEN
Anthony?

ROCKWALL
More than all right. (He goes to his desk and pulls money from the drawer) Well, Kelly, my man, it was a good bilin' of soap. Let's see, you had $5,000 in cash.

KELLY

I paid out $300 more of my own. I had to go a little above the 'stimate. I got the express wagons and cabs... (ELLEN stiffens, beginning to realize what has happened. As KELLY talks, ROCKWALL nods at her with a satisfied smile.) ...mostly for five dollars, but the trucks and two-horse teams mostly raised me to ten dollars. The motormen wanted ten dollars, and some of the loaded teams twenty dollars. The cops stuck me the hardest—fifty dollars. I paid two, and the rest twenty and twenty-five dollars. (ELLEN gasps. KELLY turns to her.) It's the coppers that always get ya. (Turns back to ROCKWALL) But didn't it work beautiful, Mr. Rockwall. I wouldn't want no Hollywood movie director onto that little outdoor vehicle mob scene. I wouldn't want to break no heart with jealousy. And never a rehearsal neither! The boys was on time to the fraction of a second. It was two hours before a snake could wiggle below Greeley's[6] statue.

ROCKWALL

(Counts out money) Thirteen hundred. There you are, Kelly. Your thousand and the three hundred you were out. You don't despise the money, do you, Kelly?

KELLY

Me? I can lick the man that invented poverty. Well, Guv. I'm off to me Alice. 'Course she won't admit it, but she's my lass. (He tips his hat to ELLEN and starts to exit)

ROCKWALL

Kelly. (KELLY stops at the door) You didn't notice, anywhere in that tie-up, a kind of fat boy without any clothes on shooting arrows with a bow, did you?

KELLY

(Thinks, mystified) Why, no, I didn't. If he was like you say, maybe the cops pinched him before I got there.

ROCKWALL

I thought the little rascal wouldn't be on hand. Goodnight, Kelly.

> KELLY EXITS. ROCKWALL takes some money and riffles it under ELLEN's nose.

ROCKWALL

Unending and nonmercenary affection, huh? That was the cause of our Richard finding happiness. Sit down, sister. (SHE sits quietly, staring front) Did I ever tell you you look like a grey-haired angel that had been left on Earth by mistake? Of course, right now, my angel can't think of a word to say. (He walks back to the desk, waves money in the air) Can I buy you a new pair of wings, perhaps, or…a couple of hours?

> Suddenly, ELLEN smiles, a big, beaming smile, and then SHE laughs, a rich, joyful sound.

ROCKWALL

(Somewhat taken aback) I'm glad you're such a good sport.

ELLEN

I'm glad YOU are. (She rises) Dear Brother, that little boy. How did you describe him? Plump. A cherub with no clothes carrying a bow and arrow? I think his name is Cupid, and he symbolizes love. Not money, dear Anthony, LOVE. And of course he was not at the blockade. He didn't have to be. (She brushes at ROCKWALL's hair with her hands. She admires him.) Did I ever tell you, dear Brother, you remind me of Atlas upon whose shoulders the world is supported?

ROCKWALL

What do you mean, he didn't have to be there?

ELLEN

Can love be deterred by distance? Especially only a few blocks away? That's why Cupid didn't have to be there.

ROCKWALL

I, don't understand.

ELLEN

No, he wasn't at the blockade, because he was here, in this room. Here. (She walks to him and places her hand on his heart.) It was your love for Richard, forget the means, it was love. And Cupid didn't have to draw his bow. You see, Cupid is a very modern lad. I think you could use him in your business. He didn't have to draw his bow. He knew your love for Richard would do it for him.

ELLEN smiles. ROCKWALL ponders.

LIGHTS DOWN SLOWLY

END OF PLAY

NOTES

The Perfect Fool

1. "nabob," a provincial governor of the Mogul empire in India; a person of great wealth or prominence (www. merriam-webster.com/dictionary/nabob)

2. "buck at faro," probably a reference to the phrase "buck the tiger" associated with the game of faro played in frontier saloons. (Ron Scheer, Old West glossary, Buddies in the Saddle, buddiesinthesaddle.blogspot.com)

3. Buckle's *History of Civilization,* by Henry Thomas Buckle, English historian (1821–1862) (en.wikipedia.org/wiki/ Henry_Thomas_Buckle)

4. Septimus Winner, 1827–1902, songwriter, *Eureka Method for the Banjo in C Notation*, 1858 (books.google.com)

5. "The Two Orphans," American silent film, 1915 starring Theda Bara (en.wikipedia.org/wiki/ The_Two_Orphans_%281915_film)

The Perfect Stranger

1. "gumshoe," an old slang term for a detective or investigator (police-affiliated or private). Shoes in the late 1800s were made of gum rubber—the soft-soled precursors of the modern sneaker. The phrase "to gumshoe" meant to sneak around quietly as if wearing gumshoes. (www. urbandictionary.com/define.php?term=gumshoe)

2. *East Lynne*, refers to matinee performance of the stage play based on the book by English novelist Ellen Ward. A melodrama and tear jerker (en.wikipedia.org/wiki/ East_Lynne)

3. "opodeldoc," a camphorated liniment of soap mixed with alcohol (Ron Scheer, Old West glossary, Buddies in the Saddle, buddiesinthesaddle.blogspot.com)

The Perfect Archer

1. Eden Mussee, wax museum, 55 W23rd St, NYC, 1884–1915 (http://ephemeralnewyork.wordpress.com/2011/06/22/when-the-eden-musee-thrilled-west-23rd-street/)

2. "Nesselrode," a rich frozen pudding/pie made of chestnuts, eggs, and cream; named after Russian Count Nesselrode (www.thefreedictionary.com/Nesselrode)

3. Knickbockers was a term for Manhattan's aristocracy in the 1800s and became a general term, now obsolete, for a New Yorker. (en.wikipedia.org/wiki/Knickerbockers)

4. Wallacks Theater, 23rd St, NYC, closed in 1915.

5. "burn a few punk sticks in the joss house to the great god Mazuma," a punk stick is a kind of incense, "joss hoss" or "joss house" is a reference to a Chinese temple, and "mazuma" is a Yiddish nickname for money (en.wikipedia.org/wiki/Joss_house; www.thefreedictionary.com/mazuma)

6. "Greeley's statue," Horace Greeley 1811–1872, newspaper publisher, statue executed 1890 by John Quincy Ward, in front of now demolished Tribune Building at Herald Square, moved to City Hall Park in 1916. (en.wikipedia.org/wiki/Herald_Square)

The Gift Of The Magi

by O. Henry, adapted for the stage by David J. Mauriello

A Full-Length Musical

Book by David J. Mauriello; Lyrics and Music by Robert Johnson

O'Henry's CLASSIC CHRISTMAS story of love and self-sacrifice.

Can be performed with a cast of six playing multiple roles, or full ensemble. Piano, or small musical combo. Suitable for all ages, and venues including dinner theater.

"Magical." *~The Humboldt Beacon*

"Delight to the senses." *~The Times Standard*

Available for licensing.

www.davidjmauriello.com

Reminders of Home

by David J. Mauriello

FORTHCOMING in 2014 - NEWLY REVISED EDITION

Originally published in 2002

Imagine that you have a great treasure and you hide it for safekeeping. Then you get amnesia! Wouldn't you welcome someone or something that would show you how to remember where your treasure is?

REMINDERS OF HOME is a *how to* book. The treasure you will find is inside you, something you may have forgotten, your true, wonderful SELF.

www.ingramcontent.com/pod-product-compliance
Lightning Source LLC
Chambersburg PA
CBHW060135260626
47160CB00005B/2118